MW00988259

The Best of
Success

Compiled by
Katherine Karvelas
Successories, Inc., Editorial Coordinator

CAREER PRESS
3 Tice Road, P. O. Box 687
Franklin Lakes, NJ 07417
1-800-CAREER-1; 201-848-0310 (NJ and outside U. S.)
FAX: 201-848-1727

THE BEST OF SUCCESS
Cover design by Successories
Typesetting by Eileen Munson
Printed in the U.S.A. by Book-mart Press

To order this title, please call toll-free 1-800-CAREER-1 (NJ and Canada: 201-848-0310) to order using VISA or MasterCard, or for further information on books from Career Press.

Library of Congress Cataloging-in-Publication Data

The best of success : quotations to illuminate the journey to success
/ by editors of Successories.
    p.   cm.
  ISBN 1-56414-386-4 (pbk.)
  1. Success--Psychological aspects--Quotations, maxim, etc.
I. Successories, Inc.
BF637.S8B466   1998
158.1--dc21   98-29821

Table of Contents
The Best of Success

Introduction

The search for personal and professional success is a lifelong journey of trial and error. This inspiring collection of wit and wisdom is a celebration of life's lessons. Each saying is a motivational push to stay on track of your goals and pursue your dreams.

In these pages you will find more than 300 powerful and compelling quotations from a diverse group of people—business professionals, writers, activists, actors, artists, sports professionals, scientists, philosophers, politicians, and everyday people who inspire us.

This unique collection was compiled after years of insightful reading and warm discussions with people who were kind enough to share their personal collections of quotations. Working on this book has been an enlightening and gratifying experience. We hope reading these quotes will be an equally gratifying and motivating experience for you on your journey of success.

Belief

Belief consists in accepting the affirmations of the soul; unbelief, in denying them.

Ralph Waldo Emerson

These, then, are my last words to you: Be not afraid of life. Believe that life is worth living and your life is worth living and your belief will help create the fact.

William James

Human beliefs, like all other
natural growths, elude the barrier
of systems.

George Eliot

Strong beliefs win strong men, and
then make them stronger.

Walter Bagehot

If a man hasn't discovered
something that he would die
for, he isn't fit to live.

Martin Luther King, Jr.

Belief

If you do not believe in yourself,
very few other people will.

Anonymous

To accomplish great things, we
must not only act, but also dream;
not only plan, but also believe.

Anatole France

To succeed, we must first believe
that we can.

Michael Korda

What the mind of man can
conceive and believe, the mind
of man can achieve.

W. Clement Stone

Sooner or later, those who win are
those that think they can.

Richard Bach

The thing always happens that you
really believe in; and the belief in a
thing makes it happen.

Frank Lloyd Wright

Y*ou have to believe in yourself. And you have to, down deep within the bottom of your soul, feel that you can do the job that you've set out to do.*

William Castle DeVries

The only limit to our realization of
tomorrow will be our doubts of
today.

Franklin D. Roosevelt

One person with a belief is equal to
a force of ninety-nine who have
only interests.

John Stuart Mill

People may doubt what you say, but
they will believe what you do.

Anonymous

I don't think anything is unrealistic
if you believe you can do it.

Mike Ditka

The very act of believing creates
strength of its own.

Anonymous

The future belongs to those who
believe in the beauty of their
dreams.

Eleanor Roosevelt

What distinguishes the majority of
men from the few is their inability
to act according to their beliefs.

Henry Miller

No man is happy unless he
believes he is.

Syrus

Success is a state of mind. If you
want success, start thinking of
yourself as a success.

Anonymous

The only thing that stands between a man and what he wants from life is often merely the will to try it and the faith to believe that it is possible.

Richard M. De Vos

Those who say it can't be done
are usually interrupted by others
doing it.

Joel A. Barker

Man is what he believes.

Anton Chekhov

As I get older I seem to believe less
and less and yet to believe what I
do believe more and more.

David Jenkins

Everybody keeps telling me how surprised they are with what I've done. But I'm telling you honestly that it doesn't surprise me. I knew I could do it.

Patrick Ewing

Nothing splendid has ever been achieved except for those who dare to believe that something inside of them was superior to circumstance.

Bruce Barton

Courage

Courage is the first of human
qualities because it is the quality
which guarantees all others.

Winston Churchill

Whatever you do, you need courage. Whatever course you decide upon, there is always someone to tell you that you are wrong. There are always difficulties arising that tempt you to believe your critics are right. To map out a course of action and follow it to an end requires some of the same courage that a soldier needs. Peace has its victories, but it takes brave men and women to win them.

Ralph Waldo Emerson

Courage is the price that life exacts
for granting peace.

Amelia Earhart

The courage to imagine the
otherwise is our greatest resource,
adding color and suspense to all
our life.

Daniel J. Boorstin

Courage is being scared to
death—but saddling up anyway.

John Wayne

One man with courage makes a majority.

Andrew Jackson

Courageous risks are life giving. They help you grow, make you brave and better than you think you are.

Joan L. Curcio

What would life be if we had no courage to attempt anything?

Vincent Van Gogh

Everyone has talent; what is rare is
the courage to follow the talent to
the dark place where it leads.

Erica Jong

To have character is to be big
enough to take life on.

Mary Caroline Richards

It takes as much courage to have
tried and failed as it does to have
tried and succeeded.

Anne Morrow Lindbergh

I love the man that can smile in trouble, that can gather strength from distress, and grow brave by reflection. 'Tis the business of little minds to shrink; but he whose heart is firm, and whose conscience approves his conduct, will pursue his principles unto death.

Thomas Paine

Courage is the ladder on which all
the other virtues mount.

Clare Boothe Luce

Wherever you see a successful
business, someone once made a
courageous decision.

Peter Drucker

Little minds attain and are
subdued by misfortunes; but
great minds rise above them.

Washington Irving

Courage is the capacity to confront what can be imagined.

Leo Rosten

The pressure of adversity does not affect the mind of the brave man…it is more powerful than external circumstances.

Seneca

Life shrinks or expands in proportion to one's courage.

Anaïs Nin

Perfect courage means doing
unwitnessed what we would be
capable of with the world looking
on.

Francois de la Rochefoucauld

Courage is grace under pressure.

Ernest Hemmingway

The greatest test of courage on
the earth is to bear defeat without
losing heart.

R. G. Ingersoll

Y*ou can gain strength, courage, and confidence by every experience in which you really stop to look fear in the face....You must do the thing which you think you cannot do.*

Eleanor Roosevelt

What a new face courage puts on everything!

Ralph Waldo Emerson

Good ideas are not adopted automatically. They must be driven into practice with courageous impatience.

Hyman G. Rickover

The best way out is always through.

Robert Frost

The bravest are surely those who have the clearest vision of what is before them, glory and danger alike, and yet notwithstanding, go out to meet it.

Thucydides

Courage is not the absence of fear, but rather the judgment that something else is more important than fear.

Ambrose Redmoon

Goals

The ultimate goal should be doing
your best and enjoying it.

Anonymous

Think and feel yourself there!
To achieve any aim in life, you
need to project the end-result.
Think of the elation, the
satisfaction, the joy! Carrying
the ecstatic feeling will bring
the desired goal into view.

Grace Speare

Nothing can resist the human will
that will stake even its existence on
its stated purpose.

Benjamin Disraeli

It takes a person with a mission to
succeed.

Clarence Thomas

It's never finished. There's always
the next objective, the next goal.

Moya Lear

The great and glorious
masterpiece of man is how to
live with a purpose.

Michel de Montaigne

Success is the progressive
realization of a worthy goal or
ideal.

Earl Nightingale

The person who makes a success
of living is the one who sees his
goal steadily and aims for it
unswervingly. That is dedication.

Cecil B. DeMille

The most important thing is to have a code of life, to know how to live. Find yourself a port of destination.

Dr. Hans Seyle

An aim in life is the only fortune worth finding.

Jacqueline Kennedy Onassis

Setting a goal is not the main thing. It is deciding how you will go about achieving it and staying with that plan.

Tom Landry

O*ur goals can only be reached through a vehicle of a plan, in which we must fervently believe, and upon which we must vigorously act. There is no other route to success.*

Stephen A. Brennan

You must be single-minded. Drive
for the one thing on which you
have decided.

George S. Patton

You have to have a dream so you
can get up in the morning.

Billy Wilder

Think little goals and expect little
achievements. Think big goals and
win big success.

David Joseph Schwartz

Unless you give yourself to some
great cause, you haven't even
begun to live.

William P. Merrill

What's important is that one strives
to achieve a goal.

Ronald Reagan

We must walk consciously only part
way toward our goal, and then leap
in the dark to our success.

Henry David Thoreau

Success is focusing the full power
of all you are on what you have a
burning desire to achieve.

Wilfred A. Peterson

It's time to start living the life we've
imagined.

Henry James

Singleness of purpose is one of the
chief essentials for success in life,
no matter what may be one's aim.

John D. Rockefeller

You have to set the goals that are almost out of reach. If you set a goal that is attainable without much work or thought, you are stuck with something below your true talent and potential.

Steve Garvey

The tragedy of life doesn't lie in not reaching your goal. The tragedy lies in having no goal to reach.

Benjamin Mays

Having a goal is a state of happiness.

E. J. Bartek

There is one thing which gives radiance to everything. It is the idea of something around the corner.

G. K. Chesterton

Purpose is what gives life a meaning.

C. H. Parkhurst

If you set a goal for yourself and are able to achieve it, you have won your race. Your goal can be to come in first, to improve your performance, or just finish the race—it's up to you.

Dave Scott

We must do the best we can with what we have.

Edward Rowland Sill

Excellence

Excellence is doing ordinary things
extraordinarily well.

John W. Gardner

If a man is called to be a streetsweeper, he should sweep streets even as Michelangelo painted, or Beethoven composed music, or Shakespeare wrote poetry. He should sweep streets so well that all the hosts of heaven and earth will pause to say, here lived a great streetsweeper who did his job well.

Martin Luther King, Jr.

I use nothing but the best ingredients. My cookies are always baked fresh. I price cookies so that you cannot make them at home for any less. And I still give cookies away.

Debbi Fields

Anybody who accepts mediocrity—in school, on the job, in life—is a person who compromises, and when the leader compromises, the whole organization compromises.

Charles Knight

Do not wish to be anything but what you are, and try to be that perfectly.

St. Francis de Sales

Excellence is the gradual result of always striving to do better.

Pat Riley

If we want to make something really superb on this planet, there is nothing whatever that can stop us.

Shepherd Mead

Always do your best. What you
plant now, you will harvest later.

Og Mandino

I never had a policy; I have just
tried to do my very best each and
every day.

Abraham Lincoln

Do your work; not just your work
and no more, but a little more for
the lavishing's sake—that little
more which is worth all the rest.

Dean Briggs

To do the right thing, at the right time, in the right way; to do some things better than they were ever done before; to eliminate errors; to know both sides of the question; to be courteous; to be an example; to work for the love of work; to anticipate requirements; to develop resources; to recognize no impediments; to master circumstances; to act from reason rather than rule; to be satisfied with nothing short of perfection.

Marshall Field & Company

We distinguish the excellent man
from the common man by saying
that the former is the one who
makes great demands on himself,
and the latter who makes no
demands on himself.

Jose Ortega y Gasset

Make it a life-rule to give your
best to whatever passes through
your hands. Stamp it with your
manhood. Let superiority be your
trademark.

Orison Swett Marden

He who has put a good finish to
his undertaking is said to have
placed a golden crown to the
whole.

Eustachius

Good enough never is.

Debbi Fields

If something is exceptionally
well-done it has embedded in its
very existence the aim of lifting
the common denominator rather
than catering to it.

Edward Fischer

If I play my best, I can win
anywhere in the world against
anybody.

Ray Floyd

The real contest is always between
what you've done and what you're
capable of doing. You measure
yourself against yourself and
nobody else.

Geoffrey Gaberino

Excellence is rarely found, more
rarely valued.

Goethe

It is those who have this
imperative demand for the best
in their natures, and who will
accept nothing short of it, that
holds the banners of progress,
that set the standards, the ideals,
for others.

Orison Swett Marden

One of the most essential things
you need to do for yourself is to
choose a goal that is important to
you. Perfection does not exist—you
can always do better and you can
always grow.

Les Brown

You always have to give 100 percent,
because if you don't, someone,
someplace, will give100 percent
and will beat you when you meet.

Ed Macauley

Much good work is lost for the lack
of a little more.

Edward H. Harriman

The quality of expectations
determines the quality of our
actions.

Andre Godin

You have to create a track record
of breaking your own mold, or at
least other people's idea of that
mold.

William Hurt

Desire

Desire, like the atom, is explosive
with creative force.

Paul Vernon Buser

A *desire to be observed,*
considered, esteemed, praised,
beloved, and admired by his
fellows is one of the earliest
as well as the keenest
dispositions discovered in
the heart of man.

John Adams

Tell me what you like and I'll tell
you what you are.

John Ruskin

You learned that, whatever you
are doing in life, obstacles don't
matter very much. Pain or other
circumstances can be there, but if
you want to do a job bad enough,
you'll find a way to get it done.

Jack Youngblood

You gotta be hungry!

Les Brown

I honestly believed I would make it. I had the desire. A lot of people have the ability, but they don't put forth the effort.

Joe Carter

No matter how old you get, if you can keep the desire to be creative, you're keeping the man-child alive.

John Cassavetes

If you really want something you can figure out how to make it happen.

Cher

Desire! That's the one secret of
every man's career. Not education.
Not being born with hidden
talents. Desire.

Bobby Unser

Desire creates the power.

Raymond Holliwell

Plant the seed of desire in your
mind and it forms a nucleus with
power to attract to itself everything
needed for its fulfillment.

Robert Collier

The starting point of all achievement is desire. Keep this constantly in mind. Weak desires bring weak results, just as a small amount of fire makes a small amount of heat.

Napoleon Hill

Dreams do come true, if we only wish hard enough. You can have anything in life if you will sacrifice everything else for it.

Sir James M. Barrie

Know what you want. Become your real self.

David Harold Fink

To educate the intelligence is to expand the horizon of its wants and desires.

James Russell Lowell

Desires are the pulses of the soul;
as physicians judge by the appetite,
so may you by desires.

Manton

It's not who jumps the highest—it's
who wants it the most.

Buck Williams

Every human mind is a great
slumbering power until awakened
by a keen desire and by definite
resolution to do.

Edgar F. Roberts

Why not spend some time
determining what is worthwhile
for us, and then go after that?

William Ross

The first principle of success is
desire—knowing what you want.
Desire is the planting of your seed.

Robert Collier

If a man constantly aspires is he
not elevated?

Henry David Thoreau

You can have anything you want if you want it desperately enough. You must want it with an inner exuberance that erupts through the skin and joins the energy that created the world.

Sheila Graham

All human activity is prompted by
desire.

Bertrand Russell

Just what you want to be, you will
be in the end.

Justin Hayward

An intense anticipation itself
transforms possibility into reality;
our desires being often but
precursors of the things which we
are capable of performing.

Samuel Smiles

One must not lose desires. They are mighty stimulants to creativeness, to love, and to long life.

Alexander Bogomoletz

You will become as small as your controlling desire; as great as your dominant aspiration.

James Allen

If you greatly desire something, have the guts to stake everything on obtaining it.

Brendan Francis

Honesty

The elegance of honesty needs no adornment.

Merry Browne

Be true to your own act
and congratulate yourself if
you have done something
strange and extravagant to
break the monotony of a
decorous age.

Ralph Waldo Emerson

Truth is a torch that shines through
the fog without dispelling it.

Claude A. Helvétius

Truth, when not sought after,
rarely comes to light.

Oliver Wendell Holmes

Learn to see things as they really
are, not as we imagine they are.

Vernon Howard

If it is not right do not do it; if it is
not true do not say it.

Marcus Aurelius

Whenever you have truth it must
be given with love, or the message
and the messenger will be rejected.

Gandhi

You never find yourself until you
face the truth.

Pearl Bailey

The pursuit of truth will set you
free; even if you never catch up
with it.

Clarence Darrow

Time is precious, but truth is more
precious than time.

Benjamin Disraeli

A man that seeks truth and loves it
must be reckoned precious to any
human society.

Epictetus

N o man, for any considerable period, can wear one face to himself, and another to the multitude, without finally getting bewildered as to which may be true.

Nathaniel Hawthorne

Telling someone the truth is a
loving act.

Mal Pancoast

Make yourself an honest man, and
then you may be sure there is one
less rascal in the world.

Thomas Carlyle

There is no twilight zone of honesty
in business. A thing is right or it's
wrong. It's black or it's white.

John F. Dodge

Being entirely honest with oneself
is a good exercise.

Sigmund Freud

It is unfortunate, considering that
enthusiasm moves the world, that
so few enthusiasts can be trusted to
speak the truth. The great seal of
truth is simplicity.

Herman Boerhaave

Peace if possible, but truth at any
rate.

Martin Luther

Always tell the truth—it's the
easiest thing to remember.

David Mamet

Honesty is the best policy, but
insanity is a better defense.

Steve Landesberg

I would give no thought of what
the world might say of me, if I
could only transmit to posterity the
reputation of an honest man.

Sam Houston

I *have found that being honest*
is the best technique I can use.
Right up front, tell people what
you're trying to accomplish and
what you're willing to sacrifice
to accomplish it.

Lee Iacocca

No one is wise or safe, but they
that are honest.

Sir Walter Raleigh

To make your children capable
of honesty is the beginning of
education.

John Ruskin

Every man who says frankly and
fully what he thinks is doing a
public service.

Leslie Stephen

Be true to your work, your word,
and your friend.

Henry David Thoreau

We must make the world honest
before we can honestly say to our
children that honesty is the best
policy.

George Bernard Shaw

Some people are likeable in spite
of their unswerving integrity.

Don Marquis

Imagination

Imagination is not a talent of some men but is the health of every man.

Ralph Waldo Emerson

First comes thought; then organization of that thought, into ideas and plans; then transformation of those plans into reality. The beginning, as you will observe, is in your imagination.

Napoleon Hill

Image creates desire. You will what
you imagine.

J. G. Gallimore

The entrepreneur is essentially a
visualizer and an actualizer. He can
visualize something, and when he
visualizes it he sees exactly how to
make it happen.

Robert L. Schwartz

Imagination decides everything.

Blaise Pascal

Our imagination is the only limit
to what we can hope to have in the
future.

Charles Kettering

Imagination is more important
than knowledge.

Albert Einstein

The man who has no imagination
has no wings.

Muhammad Ali

Reason can answer questions, but imagination has to ask them.

Ralph Gerard

The quality of the imagination is to flow and not to freeze.

Ralph Waldo Emerson

The hardest struggle of all is to be something different from what the average man is.

Charles M. Schwab

I never hit a shot, not even in practice, without having a very sharp, in-focus picture of it in my head. First I see the ball where I want it to finish, nice and white and sitting up high on the bright green grass. Then the scene quickly changes, and I see the ball going there: its path, trajectory, and shape, even its behavior on landing. Then there is a sort of fade-out, and the next scene shows me making the kind of swing that will turn the previous images into reality.

Jack Nicklaus

It takes as much imagination to
create debt as to create income.

Leonard Orr

The imagination equips us to
perceive reality when it is not fully
materialized.

Mary Caroline Richards

One who has imagination without
learning has wings without feet.

Joseph Joubert

Imagination rules the world.

Napoleon

Imagination is the beginning of creation. You imagine what you desire; you will what you imagine; and at last you create what you will.

George Bernard Shaw

Celebrate what you want to see more of.

Thomas J. Peters

Pictures help you to form the
mental mold.

Robert Collier

The imagination is never
governed, it is always the ruling
and divine power.

John Ruskin

Imagination gallops; judgment
merely walks.

Anonymous

W*hen you think something,*
you think in picture. You don't
think a thought in words. You
think a picture that expresses
your thought. Working with this
picture will produce it into your
experience.

Grace Speare

Peak performers develop powerful
mental images of the behavior that
will lead to the desired results.
They see in their mind's eye the
result they want, and the actions
leading to it.

Charles A. Garfield

We live by our imagination, our
admiration, and our sentiments.

Ralph Waldo Emerson

If everyone is thinking alike then
somebody isn't thinking.

George S. Patton

You must first clearly see a thing in
your mind before you can do it.

Alex Morrison

Love is the triumph of imagination
over intelligence.

H. L. Mencken

Love

Love is the master key which opens
the gates of happiness.

Oliver Wendell Holmes

When we understand that man is the only animal who must create meaning, who must open a wedge into neutral nature, we already understand the essence of love. Love is the problem of an animal who must find life, create a dialogue with nature in order to experience his own being.

Ernest Becker

Love sought is good, but given
unsought is better.

William Shakespeare

One word frees us of all the weight
and pain of life: That word is love.

Sophocles

Love is an act of endless
forgiveness, a tender look which
becomes a habit.

Peter Ustinov

To love deeply in one direction
makes us more loving in all others.

Madame Swetchine

Treasure the love you receive above
all. It will survive long after your
gold and good health have
vanished.

Og Mandino

When love and skill work together,
expect a masterpiece.

John Ruskin

Real success is finding your
lifework in the work that you love.

David McCullough

Love one another and you will be
happy. It's as simple and as difficult
as that.

Michael Leunig

Go to the truth beyond the mind.
Love is the bridge.

Stephen Levine

Love is a force more formidable than any other. It is invisible—it cannot be seen or measured, yet it is powerful enough to transform you in a moment, and offer you more joy than any material possession could.

Barbara De Angelis

Honor the ocean of love.

George De Benneville

For one human being to love
another; that is perhaps the most
difficult of all our tasks, the
ultimate, the last test and proof,
the work for which all other work is
but preparation.

Rainer Maria Rilke

The sweetest joy, the wildest woe is
love.

Pearl Bailey

Love, while you are able to love.

A. Frieligrath

There is a law that man should love his neighbor as himself. In a few hundred years it should be as natural to mankind as breathing or the upright gait; but if he does not learn it he must perish.

Alfred Adler

To love is to receive a glimpse of heaven.

Anonymous

Oh, love is real enough; you will
find it someday, but it has one
archenemy—and that is life.

Jean Anouilh Ardeler

Wicked men obey from fear; good
men, from love.

Aristotle

Not all of us have to possess
earthshaking talent. Just common
sense and love will do.

Myrtle Auvil

Love, by its very nature, is unworldly, and it is for this reason rather than its rarity that it is not only apolitical but anti-political, perhaps the most powerful of all anti-political human forces.

Hannah Arendt

You can give without loving, but
you cannot love without giving.

Amy Carmichael

Everybody forgets the basic thing;
people are not going to love you
unless you love them.

Pat Carroll

Love means to love that which is
unlovable; or it is no virtue at all.

G. K. Chesterton

Whenever you are confronted with an opponent, conquer him with love.

Gandhi

Love is the river of life in the world.

Henry Ward Beecher

Love cures people—both the ones who give it and the ones who receive it.

Karl A. Menninger

Opportunity

Opportunity dances with those
who are ready on the dance floor.

H. Jackson Brown, Jr.

If you want to succeed in the world you must make your own opportunities as you go on. The man who waits for some seventh wave to toss him on dry land will find that the seventh wave is a long time a-coming. You can commit no greater folly than to sit by the roadside until someone comes along and invites you to ride with him to wealth or influence.

John B. Gough

Sometimes only a change of
viewpoint is needed to convert a
tiresome duty into an interesting
opportunity.

Alberta Flanders

A wise man will make more
opportunities than he finds.

Francis Bacon

Be ready when opportunity comes.
Luck is the time when preparation
and opportunity meet.

Roy D. Chapin, Jr.

If you view all the things that happen to you, both good and bad, as opportunities, then you operate out of a higher level of consciousness.

Les Brown

Make the iron hot by striking it.

Oliver Cromwell

We see the brightness of a new page where everything yet can happen.

Rainer Maria Rilke

Take a lesson from the mosquito.
She never waits for an opening—she
makes one.

Kirk Kirkpatrick

Great opportunities to help others
seldom come, but small ones
surround us daily.

Sally Koch

Opportunities are usually disguised
as hard work, so most people don't
recognize them.

Ann Landers

There is only one optimist. He has been here since man has been on this earth, and that is "man" himself. If we hadn't had such a magnificent optimism to carry us through all these things, we wouldn't be here. We have survived it on our optimism.

Edward Steichen

The pessimist sees difficulty in every opportunity. The optimist sees the opportunity in every difficulty.

Winston Churchill

Enlarge the opportunity and the person will expand to fill it.

Eli Ginzberg

The people who get on in this world are the people who get up and look for circumstances they want, and, if they can't find them, make them.

George Bernard Shaw

Some men go through a forest and
see no firewood.

English proverb

A good deal happens in a man's
life that he isn't responsible for.
Fortunate openings occur; but it
is safe to remember that such
"breaks" are occurring all the time,
and other things being equal, the
advantage goes to the man who is
ready.

Lawrence Downs

There is far more opportunity than there is ability.

Thomas Edison

Our opportunities to do good are our talents.

Cotton Mather

Wherever there is danger, there lurks opportunity; whenever there is opportunity, there lurks danger. The two are inseparable. They go together.

Earl Nightingale

What is opportunity, and when does it knock? It never knocks. You can wait a whole lifetime, listening, hoping, and you will hear no knocking. None at all. You are opportunity, and you must knock on the door leading to your destiny. You prepare yourself to recognize opportunity, to pursue and seize opportunity as you develop the strength of your personality, and build a self-image with which you are able to live—with your self-respect alive and growing.

Maxwell Maltz

People think that at the top there isn't much room. They tend to think of it as an Everest. My message is that there is tons of room at the top.

Margaret Thatcher

A wise man doesn't just wait for the right opportunity. He creates the right opportunity. Do not wait for ideal circumstances nor for the best opportunities; they will never come.

Anonymous

Opportunity is ever worth
expecting; let your hook be ever
hanging ready, the fish will be in
the pool where you least imagine
it to be.

Anonymous

One of the earliest lessons I
learned as a child was that if you
looked away from something, it
might not be there when you
looked back.

John Edgar Wideman

Persistence

Persistence is to the character of
man as carbon is to steel.

Napoleon Hill

Nothing in the world can take
the place of persistence. Talent will
not; nothing is more common than
unsuccessful men with talent.
Genius will not; unrewarded
genius is almost a proverb.
Education will not; the world is
full of educated derelicts.
Persistence and determination
alone are omnipotent.

Calvin Coolidge

It's not so important who starts the
game but who finishes it.

John Wooden

The difference between
perseverance and obstinacy is
that one often comes from a
strong will, and the other from
a strong won't.

Henry Ward Beecher

There's only one way you can fail,
and that's to quit.

Brian Hays

I am a slow walker, but I never walk backwards.

Abraham Lincoln

You become a champion by fighting one more round. When things are tough, you fight one more round.

James J. Corbett

We can do anything we want to do if we stick to it long enough.

Helen Keller

I'm proof that great things can happen to ordinary people if they work hard and never give up.

Orel Hershiser

Many of life's failures are people who did not realize how close they were to success when they gave up.

Thomas Edison

Never give up. Keep your thoughts and your mind always on the goal.

Tom Bradley

History has demonstrated that the most notable winners usually encountered heartbreaking obstacles before they triumphed. They won because they refused to become discouraged by their defeats.

B. C. Forbes

Never despair, keep pushing on!

Sir Thomas Lipton

Permanence, perseverance,
and persistence in spite of all
obstacles, discouragements, and
impossibilities: It is this, that in all
things, distinguishes the strong
soul from the weak.

Thomas Carlyle

You are never a loser until you quit
trying.

Mike Ditka

Quit now, you'll never make it. If you disregard this advice, you'll be halfway there.

David Zucker

Some men give up their designs when they have almost reached the goal; while others, on the contrary, obtain a victory by exerting, at the last moment, more vigorous efforts than ever before.

Herodotus

You may have to fight a battle
more than once to win it.

Margaret Thatcher

You just keep pushing. You just
keep pushing. I made every
mistake that could be made. But
I just kept pushing.

Rene Mcpherson

The only way to overcome is to
hang on.

Dan O'Brien

The miracle, or the power, that elevates the few is to be found in their industry, application, and perseverance under the prompting of a brave, determined spirit.

Mark Twain

It's always too soon to quit.

David T. Scoates

The difference between a
successful person and others is
not a lack of strength, not a lack
of knowledge, but rather a lack
of will.

Vince Lombardi

I am confident. I never give up.

Arantxa Sanchez Vicario

I never gave up, even when people told me I'd never make it.

Bob Wickman

It's a little like wrestling a gorilla. You don't quit when you're tired, you quit when the gorilla is tired.

Robert Strauss

We are made to persist. That's how we find out who we are.

Tobias Wolff

**These other Successories® titles are available
from Career Press:**

➤ *The Magic of Motivation*

➤ *The Essence of Attitude*

➤ *The Power of Goals*

➤ *Commitment to Excellence*

➤ *Winning with Teamwork*

To order call: 1-800-CAREER-1

These other Successories® titles are available from Career Press:

- ➤ *Great Little Book on The Gift of Self-Confidence*
- ➤ *Great Little Book on The Peak Performance Woman*
- ➤ *Great Little Book on Mastering Your Time*
- ➤ *Great Little Book on Effective Leadership*
- ➤ *Great Little Book on Personal Achievement*
- ➤ *Great Little Book on Successful Selling*
- ➤ *Great Little Book on Universal Laws of Success*

- ➤ *Great Quotes from Great Women*
- ➤ *Great Quotes from Great Sports Heroes*
- ➤ *Great Quotes from Great Leaders*
- ➤ *Great Quotes from Zig Ziglar*

To order call: 1-800-CAREER-1